For Olivia

Thank you, Nana and Kurtis & Bette!

Library of Congress Cataloging-in-Publication Data

D'Amico, Carmela.

Ella the Elegant Elephant / by Carmela and Steven D'Amico.– 1st ed.   p. cm.

Summary: Ella is nervous about the first day of school in her new town, but wearing her

grandmother's good luck hat makes her feel better – until the other students

tease her and call her names.

ISBN 0-439-62792-3 – ISBN 0-439-62793-1 (alk. paper)

[1. Hats–Fiction. 2. Teasing–Fiction. 3. Moving, Household–Fiction.

4. Schools–Fiction. 5. Elephants–Fiction.] I. D'Amico, Steven. II. Title.

PZ7.D1837Ell 2004   [E]–dc22   2003028081

10 9 8 7 6 5 4   05 06 07 08

First edition, September 2004   Printed in Singapore   46

Book design by Steven D'Amico and David Saylor

The text was set in 20-point Aged.

Somewhere in the great, wide Indian Ocean lie
the Elephant Islands, hidden by a fog so thick
that no human being has ever found them.

On one of the islands lived a shy little elephant named Ella.
She loved her mother's new bakery and their cozy apartment
above it. But they were new to town and Ella was worried.

School started in only two more days.

And Ella was nervous about making new friends.

So her mother suggested that she do something
constructive, but Ella didn't know what.

"Well, there's still quite a bit of unpacking to do.
Why don't you give me a hand while we wait for
these cookies to cool?"

Ella didn't think this sounded
very fun, but she couldn't think
of anything better to do.

"Oh, all right," she said, and
followed her mother down the
creaky stairs.

The first thing Ella noticed was
a dusty, wooden hatbox.
A card taped to the top read:
TO: Ella   FROM: Grandma
Ella opened the box.
"Oh! Mom! Look!"

"Oh, yes!" her mother said. "I remember this hat very well. Grandma used to call it her 'good luck hat.' It was very special to her. I'm sure that's why she decided to give it to you."

Ella held the hat to her chest. Then she put the hat on her head.

"I love it!" she said. "I absolutely love it!"

On the first day of school, Ella looked like all
the other elephants in her class.
Except for one thing. . .

Ella wore her hat.

The teacher asked if she wouldn't mind sitting in a desk in the back row, so she wouldn't block the other students' view of the chalkboard.

When the class was settled, Miss Briggs said, "We have a new student joining us this year. Ella, will you come to the front and tell us something about yourself?"

Ella wasn't expecting this! She felt her face turn red. She took a deep breath and walked up the aisle. But on her way, she tripped and fell, landing flat on her belly!

"Belinda Blue!" scolded Miss Briggs. "I saw that! Shame on you!"

Belinda slumped down in her seat.

"I didn't mean to," she said.

At recess, Ella sat by herself,
hoping that someone might ask
her to play.
But nobody did.

Then Belinda Blue, the biggest elephant in the whole school, walked up to Ella and said, "That is a dumb hat. It doesn't even match your uniform."

"Yeah," said Belinda's friend, Tiki, pushing up her glasses. "But maybe she thinks she looks elegant in it."

Belinda shouted, "I know! Let's call her Ella the Elegant."

"Yeah!" Tiki laughed. "Ella the Elegant Elephant!"

When Ella got home from school, her mother asked how her day was.

"Terrible," Ella said. "Everyone made fun of my hat."

"Well, they must not know how special it is to you. Maybe you should tell them."

"I don't want to," Ella said. Her feelings were too hurt.

"My dearest Ella," her mother sighed. "Things will get better, I promise."

The next day at lunch, Ella sat by herself
eating her sandwich.

Then something hit her in the back of the head: a big red ball!

"Hey, Ella the Ella-gant!" shouted Belinda. "Wanna play ball?"

Ella didn't want to play ball with Belinda, but she was afraid if she didn't, she'd get teased even more. So she said, "Okay," and tossed the ball back.

But Belinda did not toss the ball back to Ella; instead she threw it on top of the safety wall that surrounded the schoolyard and said, "Well why don't you climb up and get it then?"

"But it's against the rules," said Ella.

"Nobody's looking," huffed Belinda.

"But," Ella said meekly, "I think it might be dangerous."

Belinda rolled her eyes. "No it's not dangerous. Just climb right up and throw it down. What could be more simple?"

"Well, if it's so simple," said Ella, "why don't *you* do it?"

Tiki and the others turned and looked at Belinda.

"Fine, I will." Belinda glared at Ella. "But you flunked the test."

Then she turned to her friends and shouted, "Well, don't just stand there! Help me up!"

A crowd started to gather; everyone
wondered what was going on.

So Belinda started showing off, tossing the ball
from hand to hand and hopping up and down on
just one foot.

"See how easy it is!" she exclaimed.

But in all her hopping and jumping around,
Belinda lost her balance and. . .

. . . slipped!

Nobody knew what to do!

Some of them ran off to find a teacher. Some of them covered their eyes.

But most of them just stared at her.

Belinda started to cry.

Ella felt sorry for her; maybe Belinda wasn't as tough as she seemed.

Before she had time to think about what she was doing, Ella piped up, "I'll help!"

She wasn't sure how, but she felt she had to try.

When Ella got to the top, she said, "Okay, just grab my hand."

Belinda did, and Ella started to pull with all her might. But since Ella was so small and Belinda was so big. . .

. . .Belinda's weight pulled them both over the edge!

They fell. . .

and they fell. . .

and THEN. . .

. . .something amazing happened!

Nobody – not the elephants watching from the schoolyard, not the elephants sunbathing on the beach, not even Ella or Belinda – could believe it! They were safe!

When Ella got home from school, she told her mother about the exciting events of the day.

Her mother scooped Ella up in her arms and said, "Grandma's hat must really be good luck. What you did was very brave. But you must promise me something, Ella. Promise me you will never climb the safety walls again. What happened today was magical and not likely to happen twice."

"Don't worry," Ella said. "I promise. I won't."

The next morning, Ella woke up much later than usual. She ran all the way to school, but she still didn't make it in time.

When she burst through the classroom door, she couldn't believe her eyes!

Even Belinda was smiling beneath the brim of her big purple hat!

Miss Briggs said, "Since we can't all sit in the back row, I'll have to ask you to remove your hats. . .just during class."

So everyone sat down.

And when Ella looked up at the chalkboard, she giggled. . . .

Things had definitely gotten better.